1
LEO

For the real Dr. Stan, with heartfelt thanks
for taking such good care of The Fergi
— MF

To Dr. Reich, for making my hospital visits
more fun by swapping photos of our dogs!
— KD

Tundra Books, an imprint of Penguin Random House Canada Young Readers, a Penguin Random House Company

Library and Archives Canada Cataloguing in Publication

Fergus, Maureen, author
You're in good paws / Maureen Fergus ; [illustrated by] Kathryn Durst.

Issued in print and electronic formats.
ISBN 978-0-7352-6466-3 (hardcover).—ISBN 978-0-7352-6467-0 (EPUB)

I. Durst, Kathryn, illustrator II. Title. III. Title: You are in good paws.

PS8611.E735Y68 2019 jC813'.6 C2018-906276-2
C2018-906277-0

Published simultaneously in the United States of America by Tundra Books of Northern New York, an imprint of Penguin Random House Canada Young Readers, a Penguin Random House Company

Library of Congress Control Number: 2018962667

Edited by Samantha Swenson
Designed by John Martz
The artwork in this book was created using pastel and colored pencils, and was finished digitally.
The text was set in a typeface based on hand lettering by Kathryn Durst.

Printed and bound in China

www.penguinrandomhouse.ca

1 2 3 4 5 23 22 21 20 19

YOU'RE IN GOOD PAWS

Written by
MAUREEN FERGUS

Illustrated by
KATHRYN DURST

tundra

Leo was a little nervous about getting his tonsils out.

"Don't worry, sweetheart," said his mom.
"The hospital staff will take good care of you."

"Are you sure we went in the right door?" asked Leo.

"Of course I'm sure!" laughed his dad.

Then he presented Leo to the chicken at the admissions desk.

The chicken asked Leo his name and address. She gave him and his teddy identification bracelets and flea collars. Then she introduced him to a volunteer named Jamal.

Jamal took Leo and his parents up to the pre-operative waiting area.

"Good luck with your operation, Leo," said Jamal.

"Thanks, Jamal!" said Leo.

It was a busy day in the surgery unit, so Leo played with toys and read books until the nurse clip-clopped into the waiting area and called his name.

QUILL & QUIRE
F
B
A
C
D

Nurse Lorraine took Leo and his parents into a private examination room. There, she checked Leo's height and weight.

She took his temperature and blood pressure.

She listened to his heart.

Leo was so cooperative
that when they were finished,
Nurse Lorraine called him a good boy and gave him a vigorous ear skritch.

Just then, a mouse strolled into the room.

"Hello, Leo," said the mouse. "My name is Dr. Stan.
I'll be performing your operation."

At first, Leo was worried about Dr. Stan's tiny size and lack of opposable thumbs.

But Dr. Stan was so friendly and knowledgeable that he soon put Leo at ease.

Dr. Stan explained what was going to happen before, during and after Leo's tonsillectomy.

Then he asked Leo some important health questions.

Leo answered as honestly as he could.

After Dr. Stan left to scrub his paws and get into his surgery outfit, Leo and his teddy changed into hospital gowns.

Then Nurse Lorraine helped Leo onto a stretcher, tucked his teddy in beside him and wheeled them both into the operating room.

In the operating room, Dr. Stan introduced Leo to Dr. Roberta, the anesthesiologist. Her job was to make Leo fall asleep and keep him asleep for the whole operation.

Gently placing a mask over Leo's nose and mouth, Dr. Roberta asked him to count sheep backwards.

Leo nervously began to count.

"Ten . . . nine . . . eight . . ."

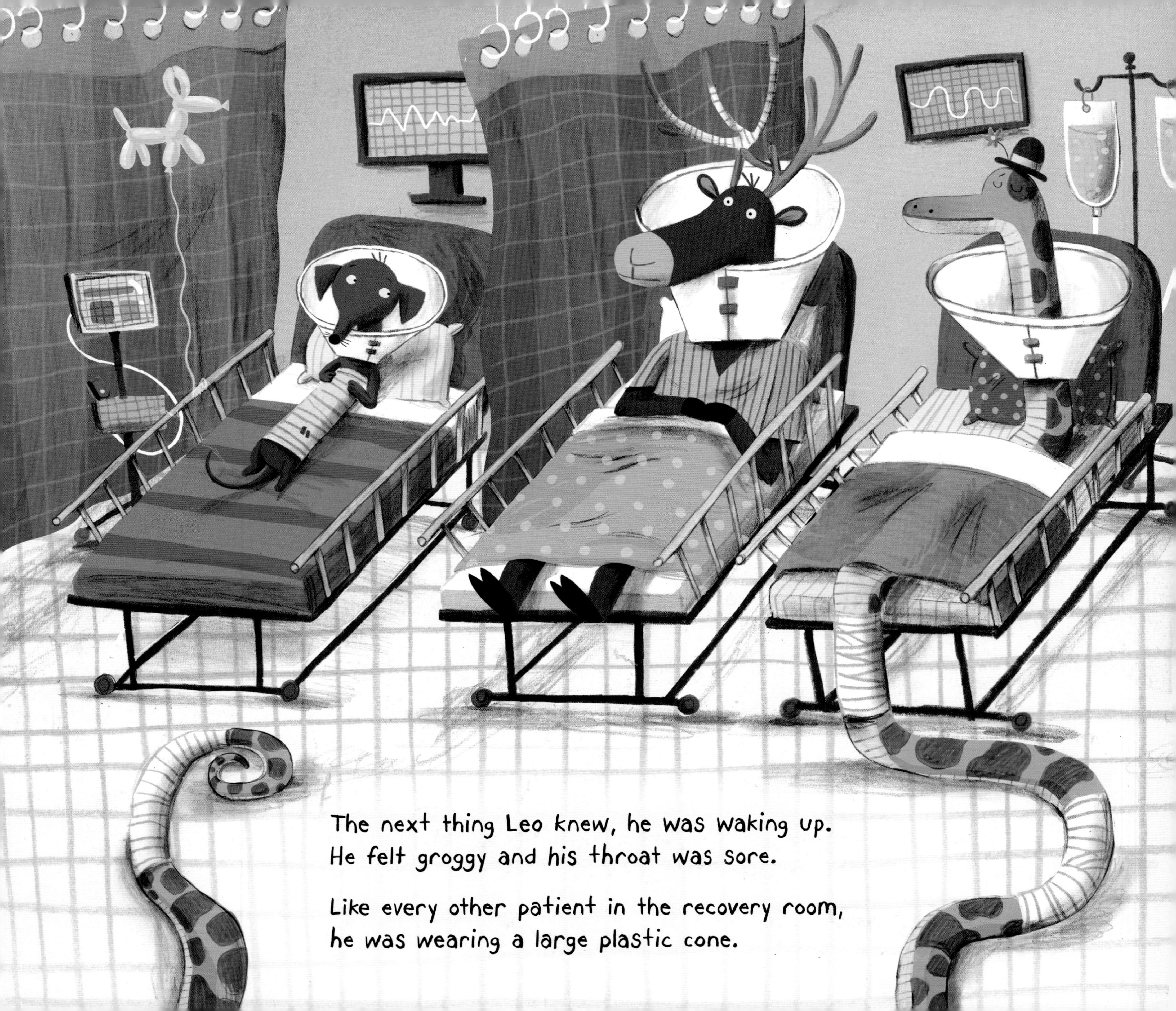

The next thing Leo knew, he was waking up.
He felt groggy and his throat was sore.

Like every other patient in the recovery room,
he was wearing a large plastic cone.

"I'll remove it if you promise not to eat anything off the floor or chew on your own leg," said Nurse Lorraine.

"I promise," rasped Leo.

Even though Leo's surgery had gone well, Dr. Stan decided to keep him in the hospital overnight for observation.

As soon as the orderly wheeled Leo into his hospital room, the patient in the other bed said, "I'm Naeem! I broke my ankle skateboarding and needed surgery to pin it back together again."

"I'm Leo," croaked Leo. "I just got my tonsils out."

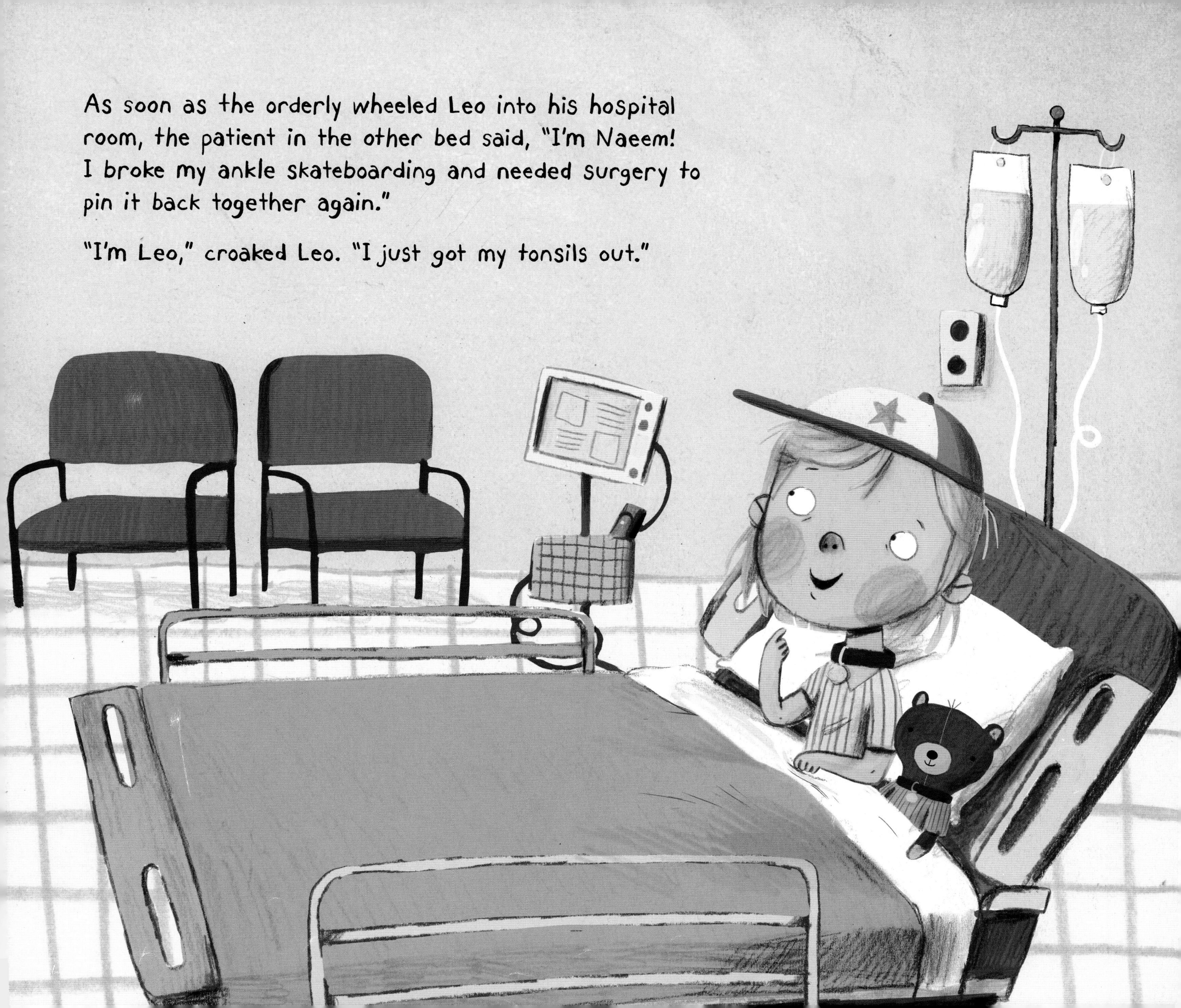

While Naeem showed Leo how to work his nifty electric bed and helped him find a cartoon station on the television, Leo's mom fetched him some ice chips and his dad got him an extra blanket.

That night, Leo had Popsicles and Jell-O for dinner.
The next day for breakfast he got ice cream AND a milkshake!

"Lucky!" cried Naeem.

After breakfast, a nurse's aide named Fifi helped Leo and Naeem wash up.

"What do you think?" asked Fifi, when she was done styling Leo's hair.

"I've never looked fluffier," said Leo politely.

Leo and Naeem spent the rest of the day watching movies, reading comics and exploring the hospital.

CAFETERIA
COMIX

Late in the day, Dr. Stan came by. After examining Leo's throat and reviewing his chart, he said Leo was officially discharged.

"Does that mean I can go home?" asked Leo.

"It certainly does," said Dr. Stan with a smile.

Leo's parents packed up his things while he shook Dr. Stan's paw, said goodbye to Naeem and thanked the hospital staff.

"My mom was right," he told them. "You DID take good care of me!"

A few weeks later, it was time for Leo to start school.

He was a little nervous, but his mom said, "Don't worry, sweetheart. Your teacher will take good care of you..."